A REVELRY OF

HARVEST

A REVELRY OF HARVEST

New and Selected Poems

Gracia Grindal

Writer's Showcase
San Jose New York Lincoln Shanghai

A REVELRY OF HARVEST
New and Selected Poems

Writer's Showcase
an imprint of iUniverse, Inc.

For information address:
iUniverse, Inc.
5220 S. 16th St., Suite 200
Lincoln, NE 68512
www.iuniverse.com

Poems previously published in:
Great River Review
College English
Dialog
Christian Century

ISBN: 0-595-21517-3

Printed in the United States of America

For my treasures
Liv Anda, Bryn Anders, Karl Theodore, Erik Haakon
Soli deo gloria

CONTENTS

Acknowledgements

Cover Art: "Valley Grove Church," Tom Maakestad ©1996. Oil Pastel 23 "x42"

DREAMS OF HOME

DREAMS

Awake. Shadows looming in the dark.
The window at my side is lighting up
with dawn, a dream has startled me. I look
out through the buzzing screen at a roof top.
A breath of salty air flutters the shade.
I have been dreaming of a gawky boy
stumbling to find his way out of my head.
I am a girl again, my longings cry
until I hear an old bicycle creak
to a halt. I feel my little sister turn
beside me. I dream I am home and wake
into another scene, the morning sun
breaks like an orange over the sleeping town
I reconstruct by shadows out of dawn.

THE FALL

One April day I lay against the ground
to watch for whooping cranes on their way south.
I gazed into the blue and then beyond.
My mother's fury flared. Back and forth
between the clotheslines and the house she'd walk
laden with rugs and clothes she wanted out
in the fresh air. She couldn't make me work—
she'd rage against me, fulminate and shout,
but I was safe in natural history,
stubborn as Eve and disobedient.
I claimed my right to know the ancient way.
Rebellion rose in me, impenitent
when mother stormed like God into the yard
and cursed me into labor with her words.

RITUAL

Memory. Its little lights flash and wink
at the edges of things. Moments of time halt:
Now I am five, kneeling beside the sink,
Mother is rinsing my hair, my tears are salt
in my mouth. I taste the vinegar. My hair
squeaks as my mother's hands wash me clean
in the cistern water. The woman does not care
for dirt. Wild as a priestess she scrubs me down.
Later she will twist my hair to snake-like curls
stabbing my head with sharp bobby pins.
I am a voodoo doll, a little girl
taking the punishment for old Eve's sins,
exorcised, made new, a miracle
I barely fathom in this ritual.

SAMUEL

I knelt beside the old and squeaky bed
on the cold linoleum floor and tried to pray.
Don't let me die, forgive me, Lord, I prayed,
and looked for revelations from the sky,
at least an angel rustling his wings,
or just a quiet voice to say, Be still.
But nothing rode the moonlight or its rings,
nothing spoke softly to my Samuel.
My god was nothing. Still, I called the name
into the cold and chilly dark. I called,
but no one answered or he would not come.
I fell into the darkness, felt the cold
against my body like a kitchen knife
held up against a bruise like Hannah's grief.

GROUND BLIZZARD

The wind shrieks in the yard, the sky is blue,
"We better go," he says, "get home before
the country roads are drifted in." We know
the road, each dip, each turn. "Go, start the car,"
she says. "I'll get the kids." She starts to bend
into the heavy task of boots and coats,
mittens and double scarves against the wind—
the miles stretch over newly drifted roads.

We venture bravely out into the cold,
the snow is riding streaks of pastel air
over the long horizon. Each snowflake holds
a diagram of frozen sun. I stare
into the white beyond the swirling drifts
at the prairie and its perishable gifts.

THE SCAR

they cut me open
and found a star
singing beneath the skin
it left a scar

the stitches tingled

if the weather turns warm
in Alaska I scratch
the storm growing on my arm

they cut one from my mother
smooth as a maple gall
and sewed the stormy weather
into her back like a ball

when the stitches broke
I fell out of her scar
all tangled up and furry
singing like a star

when her weather moves
I rain inside the bone
and feel the scar

ring on my arm like a phone

SUNDAY AFTERNOON

Father comes home
in his slave clothes
to mash potatoes
we dish up the pickles
and talk about his sermon

then we sit down
to the common meal
of Sunday dinner
roast beef seared
to a Lutheran crisp

we shut ourselves down
the quiet voyage begins
for sleep the real Sabbath
is a rest
stricter than Leviticus

we snuggle into Bible stories
ladies aids have stitched
on holy comforters for us

we fall into mythology
and sleep like lambs
in the Good Shepherd's arms

green pastures flourish
we dream between the pages
of King James Bibles
we rest in parables

of a good house
where peace is running over
and we will dwell
forever

ELISE ANDERSON, PHOTOGRAPHER, RUGBY, NORTH DAKOTA

had a hollyhock house of Bergen
goat cheese, hypo baths and blue
electric globe   I would stand
spinning the world beneath King Håkon's feet
waiting for her to leave the darkroom
and light the nations up

we homed in on Bergen

landed in the fish market
beside Edvard Grieg

stood head and shoulders
above him, tasting mackeral
salted cod, knekkebrød

crowds fussed at the small composer
he made them melodies
of great white cheese

we could not get enough
and had to leave   hungry
we sailed west
he waved good-bye
Peer Gynt singing in his eye

Duluth rose in a great lake
of harvest   we tacked our scarlet sails
home heartwound of North America

the seas she sailed me in
swirled in her sharp eye
I swam up from water
toward her   she took me out to dry
developed   the lady touched me up
she framed me   set me on her shelf
next to Grieg   we waltzed Norway
free of Swedish kings   we danced
red Norwegian flags

PRAYER MEETING IN THE UPPER ROOM IN CENTRAL LUTHERAN CHURCH, SALEM, OREGON

I grew up in seasons of prayer
listening to the deacons pray
their children good *O Father hear*
their quiet breathing and the rush
of sorrows from their sighing
they fold their hands rough and cut
from carpentry *O Father hear their prayers*
Jesus rises from them on a cloud
of paint, in a baby blue and pink sky
he is flying up in maroon bright robes
to heaven and they don't like his hands
for being hurt like theirs *Have thine own way*
potter, I am like clay
to hear the simple sentences of love
they learn to say *O Father hear them*
use heaven's tongue to measure
what they treasure here on earth
just now Lord remember
prayer moves in their muscles
from the root endings of their lives
their words beat in the pious air
hear their prayer, Lord, hear their prayer
John Vettrus breathes a soft amen
dove wings flutter over him
hover in the prayers for children
whom we do not name, Lord
and yet we name them in our hearts

Jesus, bless them
come in the grape juice and the wafers
be their guest in paper bread
feed them your food, fill their heads
with metaphors of splendor
amaze them with the grace of hands
the children of their hurting
make them wonder

PIANO LESSONS

A phrase from Brahms on the radio. A waltz.
Rustles of summer dresses in a room
filled with the scent of lilacs rise. My thoughts
go adolescent, moony, like a dream.
I see her hunch over the ivories.
She nods, closes her eyes, and starts to play
in time with me. It's Brahms. Good, she says,
keep playing, keep the beat steady, the way
your heart beats, but let each note be a surprise.
Her gold shoes tap out the time. The duet
goes on. She is lost in triple time. Her eyes
see signatures beyond my ken. I sit
watching her while she plays the distances
which lie between us, locked, inside the keys.

HAVING MISSED MY RIDE TO WORK
I READ ON THE BACKSTEPS

Out in the fields the strawberries are ripe.
I turn the pages of the book slowly.
Late, too late, I lie against the steps,
the brick red steps, reading Charlotte Bronte.
The words dance on the bright pages. Sleep,
father, my mother, deep inside the dark.
Sleep now, I've found another line of work.

Out in the fields the dew is sparkling wet,
the day is new as any girl or boy
reaching into the leaves where berries wait.
But let me read this morning secretly
stealing into the English countryside,
into the map of human love. Jane Eyre
is losing all she worked for in a fire.

My parents, falling into their morning dreams,
dream I am gone into the fields of light,
and, taking up their old familiar arms,
they will not like that I have read too late.
Out in the fields the strawberries are sweet.
I lie reading in the morning sun.
Sleep now, let me take in every one.

SPACEWALK

Once I rambled far from home
until I hit upon the sun
and plucked it from the sky
cracked sunlight from its shell
and made a meal of its meat
with milky way and dipper wine—
richly did I drink and eat.

My love rode by and spied
the shell of sun, the rind of moon
and dregs of wine.

I watched from fields of corn
his scarlet dress, his silver horn.

Only my true love could find
I whispered in the corn's ear
where I had tasted dipper wine.

I laughed and then earth fell away
beneath my silver heel

around the stars I reel and reel.

SLEEPING IN THE OLD BED WHERE MY GRANDFATHER AND HIS FATHERS BEFORE HIM WERE BORN

I lie down in the flowers
of an old tapestry
and put my face to the old designs
and sleep myself back into seed

the family patterns hold me

awake I trace the lineage back again
to my face and hands
and see the family lines
flower on my skin

I lie in a heraldry
of grace and simple kin

THE NEW LAND

Each little nook and cranny has its tale.
Here is Svein's hop, where eighty years ago
our grandfather flew like a swan over the dale
hundreds of feet above the rocks below
to save himself some time. We did not know
he was the stuff of legends left behind.
He fought stones for his children's food who grow,
nameless outcroppings in the western wind.
Back on the prairie, I would lay me down
longing to see mountains, his fragrant farm
eager to hear legends whispering around
the dish of earth I felt beneath my arms,
dreaming of stones with tales to tell, their names
mute as the bones scattered by unknown graves.

SITTING IN WESTMINSTER ABBEY THINKING OF HANS NIELSEN HAUGE CHRISTIAN PATRIOT AND EVANGELIST TO NORWAY DURING THE 18TH CENTURY

I sit in Westminster and worship God
with William Blake and Byron staring down
at priests pirouetting in their gowns
of lace and ornate crosses. Bishop Laud,
I am a Non-Conformist forced abroad
by policies of yours. I built new towns
in North Dakota, added commercial nouns
to the royal tongue. Still, I am awed.

Fancy me sitting here at evensong,
moved by the gaudy rituals of lords,
whose ancestors laid hands on any forms
beautiful enough to see. I long
to lie prostrate on stone and utter words
the shape of fire, nurtured in prairie storms.

THE HARROWING OF HELL

It is Easter in Viet Nam
soldiers are hanging from helicopters
like drunken ants

across the street
a police car stops
and flashes a spotlight on a quiet house

a worm gnaws
at the center

by Greenwich time
it is Easter
ladies in London are walking
through daffodils to church
light is streaming through stained glass
and priests intoning words
of angels by the crypt

outside the snow glazes with ice
on the radio from Cedar Rapids
someone says we should bomb
Viet Nam back to the stone age

below the ground Jesus is licking
his wounds
his head hurts and he groans
shocked by the taste of vinegar
ebbing in his throat

by now in Coventry
the angels are playing trumpets
etched in the morning sun

waves on the dark Atlantic
roll into azure green
under the early light

hell is a stone
Jesus pushes himself
through the dull rock
he crushes the difficult city
with the ball of his bruised foot

he grows until he bleeds
against the iron ground

the forecast is for snow
it is 4 o'clock
we have made it through

Jesus shivers in the cold wind
he waits for the air to dry his wings

in London there is rain
Viet Nam is blooming
like a red flower

Jesus breathes like a thief
at the front door
bells ring

morning breaks like a stained glass window
over the wide horizon

his wings flame
he stands in the rubble
of a red stone

earth quakes
down to the bedrock
the light breaks through his wings
like a monarch he rises
over the dawn
the sun, our king

VALEDICTION ON ST. LUCY'S NIGHT
(1985 O'Hare Hotel)

I

It is the deep nocturnal of the dark,
the sun, fallen from grace, goes out like fire
on the long horizon. The trees are stark
against the winter sky. Down at the core
embers are dying. Flickering shadows lurk
on the farthest edge. Light will be no more.
Deep in my northern heart, I fear the light
fading upon the edges, the western night.

It's twenty years ago this very hour
I stood in Oslo by an iron gate
watching the snow fill an empty yard,
and, flushed with triumph, looking down the street,
I saw you come for me. You were as dour
as Russia in your sheepskin and floppy hat—
you grumbled like an old man at the cold.
Young, you loathed the fact of getting old.

II

Deep in an Asian jungle, a soldier crept
toward our destruction. We were as innocent
of life as death—your rectitude slept
between us like a flaming sword. We meant

to find ourselves. The bombs went off. We kept
dreaming of Italy, the days we'd spend
in Rome or Florence, ready for light and sun,
there by the classic Mediterranean.

The soldier took dead aim. Our world blew up.
A seismic quake shifted the world we knew,
we watched the continental drift of Europe
fade from the scene and Asia swing into view.
Terra incognito, an unknown map
floated before us, uncharted, a dangerous jewel.
We thought we were different from any gone before,
the first real victims of a dirty war.

III

The airport roars and rumbles by my bed,
the sky is brilliant with the winter stars.
Out west the winter fog is dense and sad,
but I have written late and morning nears.
Words form themselves like cookies in my head.
I think of time, the rich, surprising years,
and cannot sleep. That night keeps coming back,
shadows forming themselves against the bricks.

You say we go from sunlight into dark.
It's then I think of standing by that gate,
swathed in my virtue and my brilliant work.
That light fades for me now, the hour was late,
the big bell tolled its midnight through the park,
I could not read its meaning. I would wait
until this hour, until my middle age
to scribble it darkly on this yellow page.

IV

The sun each morning for successive months,
will brighten; we are moving toward the light.
It bubbles in me like chicken soup for lunch.
The bridegroom comes, torches against the night
and light blazes forth. I waited once
and wait it still: the hope that makes us greet
each morning when the caroling robin cries
at the dawn's red gleaming in the eastern skies.

How lovely to grow old, to feel the weight
of years make every moment shimmer forth
with meanings half remembered, to feel the night
gather its pages round us, as the earth
spins in its quiet orbit, through fields of light.
I hear the music of the shadowed north,
in this, the deep midnight of day and year.
The darkest hour is over, day is near.

WALKING IN THE SNOW NEAR WASHINGTON PRAIRIE

They will find me next spring
hunched against the snow
in a quarter moon
curved like the Sybil

I want to die
for beauty
but if I kneel
I will freeze

O Lord the stars

I am walking
in a field of opals

in the white center
of stars and flakes of snow
melting on my face and hands
washing in thousands
of six-sided shapes

oracles spring from my mouth
I brush drops of water
from my face
down to miracles
where snow banks keep me warm

this is a dream

my blood is slushing
into crystals
inside my bones
the sun shines

ice bottles me up
I fall asleep
in a white drift

O Lord the stars

ON THE ROAD NEAR WELLSBURG, IOWA

The church breaks like a stone boat
sailing the heavy ground
a school of stones riding in its wake

I watch it in the rear view mirror
keel back into earth

fish with names cut in their sides
flash in the sun and go down

I stop for a school bus
a girl in a yellow dress
steps into the wind
she looks like a seed package
flying toward her house

a farmer is out in his fields
picking rocks

in every hill of corn
set a stone
stamped with the sky
let the seed flourish
in a fish eye

something is breaking up

I feel the gods moving in the seed
into the syllables of grace
out of the dark
hulls of flowers

MIDDLE AGE

My heart pounds like the drunken messenger,
Beware, beware, it says, you're nothing more
than flesh and blood, I let the passions stir
and then I hammer out, Beware, beware.
It's late. I cannot think of anything,
life ebbs in a fatty vein, like the rolling world.
The radio is jazzy with a song
we used to sing. The world is growing old,
I see it there, the crowfeet round our eyes,
the tracking of this life upon the skin.
The word, I hear a word, but what it says
sifts from me in the dark. I sing again:
death is the slow disorganizing of
the force that draws us, dreadfully, to love.

HURT

Your voice brings back the golden time,
our youth, the garden, where we fell into
losses I can only now recount, like flames
banked up inside an isolated room
in a long deserted building on a farm
that seems as dead as winter. Suddenly,
the scarlet embers flare up into the dome
of night and neighbors several miles away
notice the conflagration. The human heart
confounds me even as, lying here,
I break open like wine against the hurt
we did each other, but there it is, the scar
freshly red against the linen sheets,
and now I am old enough to say it hurts.

LOVE'S SENTENCE

I hold the cup of mercy to your lips
and hear the words you swore to me of love,
trembling with good intentions, in your cups
and false as sunlight on an icy wave.
I say the words that promise blood for wine
and suffer you to come where things are new,
where miracles are commonplace as dawn,
and what is ordinary changed. I say
the wine is blood and shed for you, my friend,
made faithless in another hour. What faith
there is between us splashes in my hand,
the nourishment we take against our death.
It's mercy that I'm holding out for you
hoping you hear the sentence as I do.

REGRET

Later, after the ice has melted down
and talk is over for a little spell
we wonder, what else we should have said or done.
Settling back in the chair, someone will smile,
"I should have left him there…I should have said…
If only I had thought to…" Regret like smoke
rises in the dusky air. It is dead,
we say about the past, but feel it lurk
beside us in the night. The characters
we play have come to grief in each of us.
But, wait, let's try that over. How young they are!
They twinkle like figures in a cave of ice.
Give them a better end, we want to say,
caught in the great Titanic of our play.

DESPOT

Pink, the color of Salem in the spring
flutters around us in the Hall of Mirrors.
This is the heart of Europe, the real thing.
The light shatters in the dusty chandeliers
behind your head. Sun king of glass and tears,
touch me and make me whole, I want to live.
Tell me the truth, the dates, the brutal years,
this is my hands-on course in Western Civ.
Outside the formal gardens wait. They give
some order to the anarchy I feel
welling like rabble in my brain, reprieve
from all the graven sentences that wheel
around us in this quaint and marble hall
where despots came to grief, trying not to fall.

BOLTS OF BLUE

They rustle through my dreams in priestly robes,
gathering like a troop of angels where
they circle around me in their heavy garb,
a ministry of uncles in my hair:
The apostolic laying on of hands.
A bolt of lightning hits from the crowded blue
and men in cutaways with tails and striped pants
murmur against me like the Pharisees.
A door slams shut. Full of electric light
I start to glow, St. Elmo in the dark.
The air crackles, the power disconnects.
I fill with a radiance that does not work.
A fuse blows, the grill is molten ash
and I go out like fireflies, in a flash.

RAPTURE

Medieval Russians at Epiphany
extinguished candles in baptismal fonts
to signify that Christ had come with fire
and water. They baptized with the Holy Ghost
and fire, loving the purifying flame.
The Old Believers, knowing they were done,
burned themselves, letting the rapture come.
The fires consumed them. Cinders, they were gone.

I'm Puritan as Cromwell at the heart
and would have gone round knocking off stone heads
waiting the Second Coming, stern and hard.
So fire is a word I comprehend, like God.
There's rapture in it, Protestant and spare
like Armageddon, earth gone up in fire.

THE WATER OF LIFE

My fever throbs, making the light in the glass
pierce like an icicle through my aching head.
I want to curl up in a ball and force
my body back into my mother's bed
and disappear from my skin, to go inside
to the deepest places in my aching bone,
my body cries like the prodigal for home.

Yesterday I walked through the stony vaults
of Chartres chilled by the dank medieval rock
seeping with old confessions, bitter faults,
bargains with God and prayers to heal the sick.
The blue windows made my temples ache
as I trudged toward Roland and his tragic horn
blasting against the pagans, for Charlemagne.

The daffodils outside bend in the wind
and the salt air is fragrant with fresh bread.
I dream like a legionnaire in parks of sand
of cups of water raising me from the dead.
Tossing and turning cathedrals in my head
the morning sun glows like neon signs.
Someone beside me is opening the blinds.

She gives me oranges, like Spanish suns,
glasses of water, drawn from crystal springs,
my angel bustles like a town at noon
burbling good news like water from her tongue.
I cannot fathom her words, I know the song.
She brings me water like a sacrifice

from sacred wells kept cold by summer ice.
I drink and am made whole, now I will live.
In a few days, like Adam, I will walk the park,
marveling at the simplest gifts we have—
sweet rain gurgling down the street by dark
glistening in the light, on the scrabbly bark,
washing away contagions, making fresh
the earth beneath, the air, all living flesh.

THE SIGN OF JONAH

I

By Lake Superior the woman writes
all night her typewriter
works like the sea.
She sits in the dark and crows
when the words come out right.

Her lover flings himself
against the wall and dry lands.
It is not right, he says
sinking into his virtue,
for me to want her now,
but I do. I want to break
into her like a thief.

II

Adam Bede falls
from my mother's hand
waking my father.
He groans at the noise:

the tack tack of keys
working against the night.

III

They aren't married, she says
rolling the berries
in her hand.

These will make good jam.

IV

Crazy for culture, she writes,
I went to Prague.
She notices my parents
gathering berries
in the wooded lot
beside the cabins.
In a word
she gets them down.

V

Different, she says, popping a berry
into her mouth. George Eliot
lived with a man like that.
The latter days.
Let's go watch the bears.

VI

The old world lives in memory,
she writes looking across
the great metallic water,
looking for a sign.

VII

At the dump the bears
perform their old routines
scavenging for food.
I wonder, she says, about the kids.

Look at the cubs, he says.

VIII

Back at the cabin they hear
the lovers fighting.
Here, let's boil these down.
I'll make jelly later.

IX

Putting cream on the raspberries
she says, that other one there,
she's a preacher's kid
from up by Hawley.

X

Words click across her page.
Minneapolis, she writes,
refuses to be mythic.

XI

We were in the Cities, she says,
we'd gone down on the Empire Builder
for the Annual Meeting.

XII

The student downstairs
walks around the house
looking for flowers
to make his girl a spring corsage.
Try the lilacs, I yell.

XIII

I found the old world in Prague,
she writes. My uncle boards
the Red River Special in Willmar.
I remember, he says,
when we used to go to town
to smoke cigarettes and talk English.

XIV

Jesus said it would be so.
She reads for her devotions:
There shall be no sign
but the sign of the prophet Jonas.

XV

a) He wants her.
   Not tonight, she writes
   like a wife.

b) Move over. The waves slap
   under the pier.
   What about the kids, she says.
   Water moves beneath them.

c) Whistling a tune I taught him
   from an old hymn book

   the young man in the basement
   sets lilacs in her hair

   lilacs I cut back
   to their roots three years ago.

MARRIAGE
(for the 35th wedding anniversary of my parents)

There they go.
We should have brass bands
for this. You can tell
he loves her when the car
stops at the stop sign,
he rubs his hand over his upper lip
and looks at her. She is
moving her hand slowly
over her white purse.
They speak to each other.
You can see roses fall
in the spaces between them.
The car brims with rose petals,
white petals whisper out the windows,
in a cloud of blossoms they drive
down the road. For this
there should be brass bands.

WATCHING AT THE AUCTION

The auctioneer is selling cut glass bowls,
dishes and stoneware crocks, singing out bids
on Mason jars with old, corroded lids,
vases for stalks of bittersweet; he strolls
to the next table, lifts a clock with scrolls
carved in its corners. Farmers, chewing quids
of dark tobacco, spit, and watch their kids
climbing on a heap of wooden poles.

Lying by the garden on an old chaise lounge
killing time and eating chocolate cake;
I see a hedge bright with rosehips. *The past,
doctor, the past, is going for a song*—
The shape of things gathers, shatters and breaks
And everything is going, going, fast.

IONA

The gladioli drop beads of water on the wood
as they are handed down into the boat
to lie upon the coffin. The man shivers
looking at the rolling sea and pulls his coat
tighter around his shoulders. "At least she'll float,"
he says, looking across the wintry sea
toward the sunlit abbey, then at me.

The last remains of Kate MacArther rest
beside us, she has followed us from Mull.
I heard the country talk as we sailed west,
over the silver whale roads through the hills.
Now we are bobbing toward the Holy Isle
four living and one dead. The water beads
on the wood, golden as a glass of mead.

The sun is setting on the abbey walls,
my Viking blood rushes to take its stand
against the Christians and their book of Kells.
They came to kill and plunder gold for bad ends,
to massacre the monks upon the sand,
and take for magic, stones set in the cross
for charms and use them for their pagan ways.

A tractor meets us at the dock and lifts
the casket out. She's home, a bonny lass
ninety years on the island. She never left
except to die. Home on the Applecross,
her people greet her without many tears,
though they have lost an old one in her death.
They speak of the loss quietly, under their breath.

"Is there," I ask a mourner standing by
"a place where I can stay a night or two?"
She points me down the street, a B & B.
The weather has turned, waves crash, greenish blue,
on to the flinty rock. I watch the crew
of the Applecross loosen the straining ropes
and wave goodbye. Above them the standard flaps.

Finding a room, I settle in. The waves
restlessly beat against the wintry pier.
The electric fire crackles like an old wood stove
There are old books about the island here,
from the Druids until Keats appeared
and caught his death of cold walking the fens
barefoot like Fergus and Columba once.

At breakfast, my hostess tells me what to see
and gives me a map as worn as a cloth rag—
telling me not the miss the final day
of Kate MacArthur. She packs an old sack
with lunch and sends me out to climb the crags
and rocks of the Holy Isle. I start at the beach
where Vikings slaughtered monks from the old church.

Due north, across the water, Fingal's cave
gapes at me like a giant's maw. It pounds
in my head, John Thompson's lessons, wave on wave—
the notes in that old piano piece will sound
long after I have shut the book, the world around
grows into memory, here on this holy isle
things connect for me. It is magical.

Turning south I brave the western edge,
through mucky cotswolds, boots sucking out of the mire,
I find myself trapped on a high rocky ledge.
The waves crashing over the rocks make the air
alive with light and color, rainbows are here,
the light is palpable and sweet to touch,
no wonder the monks were quick to build a church.

I make my way along the western coast,
until I stand at the foot of the great hill
where Columba and his men buried their boats
after they'd landed on the Holy Isle
and climbed the steeps to see if they could still
see old Ireland loom like a green stone
off to the south and west over the whale road.

They built a mission for the Scottish Picts,
venturing east with the Good News and sat
in the cold scriptorium, lining their manuscripts
with lovely flourishes, getting their values right—
the room stony with the crystal light
that dances off the sea and lively air
around me like a dancing angel choir.

Here at the middle of the island mass
a monk saw angels riding the vaults of heaven,
playing like joyful children in the skies
shimmering presences swooping in rows of seven,
filled with a joy their Lord had given.
The road is paved, a small car putters along,
I dream I hear their old, unchanging song.

And now I stand above the church on the rock
where Saint Columba mortified his flesh—

with hairshirts and the heathen vermin—his work
continued to Cromwell's time, when zealots smashed
the heads of statues, and left the abbey crushed.
Full circle now, I am a Protestant
spartan and pious, in my element.

Processing from the north, a crowd of men
in black follows the last remains of Kate.
The coffin lurches on the cart, the sun
flashes against the rolling emerald waves,
a black gash in the ground will be her grave.
Slowly they gather around the friendly stones
marked with their names and filled with Scottish bones.

The gladioli take root in the wounded dirt
as she settles in for the sleep of ageless time.
The preacher reads the ancient, final words
and she is gone to the earth from which she came,
joined with the dust, and sealed in Jesus' name.
The coffin slams into the narrow place
where Kate MacArthur waits the day of grace.

The mourners straggle over the emerald grass
walking past ancient Irish crosses of stone.
My feet are rooted in a rocky mass.
The weather swirls around me. I watch the sun
fracture in the mists around us. The sea moans,
restless and urgent beside the new dug grave.
The whale road sighs, she sinks beneath the wave.

MOTHER TONGUE

MOTHER TONGUE

bless to bless it is old English
not found elsewhere in Teutonic
derived perhaps from blood sacrifice
to mark or affect in some way
with blood or killing to consecrate
at the English conversion it took over
benedicere and the Greek root for eulogy
meaning originally speak well of
to invoke blessings on to bend
a happy combination weaving together
our roots with the blood streaked
on the door lintels we were blessed
when the dark angel passed over
to sanctify us to make holy safe
against evil I pour my blessings on you
like blood child I mark you with benedictions
and crown you with a caul I make you
safe against the evil one may your days be
happy more than that may you be blessed
among women may you be full of grace
a blessing to your mother I hold you
to my breast and feed you milk
streaked with blood I call you blessed
blessed blessed blessed

THE BABE IN CHRIST

I

She reaches for the paper with her hands.
The Gospel written there is food for her,
or rather she can tell the word she finds
before her in her mother's hand is more
than any piece of paper, it is life
and so she reaches for it with her mouth.
She wants to be like us, she wants to live.
Though she is not the first to chew on truth.
Ezekiel hungered for the holy word
even with bitterness and suffering there,
he ate it all, the crazy prophet chewed
the parchment up and tasted bitter fire
and then its sweetness filled his soul. He ate
as she did, hungry for life, she could not wait.

II

She toddles beside me, not two years old,
proud and determined she will walk alone.
The dark is filling up the stubbly fields
and high above us in the Norway pines
the western wind booms. She looks up at me
and grasps my finger tightly. "Hand," she says,
"not finger, whole hand!" With great divinity
I reach to pick her up, she cries,
"Not carry, just hand!" She spurns my proffered help,
her little feet stamp on the beaten ground.

To love her I must almost lose my grip,
letting her reach for me, letting her find
what strength there is for her within the storm
against the fatal logic of the worm.

III

She stands beside me, small evangelist,
bursting with news her mother hopes she keeps,
but what she wants to say, it will not last.
Pulling my head down to her small lips
she lets the secret out, for all to hear.
We can't help laughing, it is news, good news.
I know what's in the package, what is more,
to open it will still be a surprise.
She did not give a thing away, she gave
a word that bound us in a pleasant room,
a house of laughter, filled with words that live
in expectation of another home
prepared for us by one whose body dwells
within us like the secret that she tells.

IV

Her little feet trip on the carpet floor
and then her voice, like any watcher cries,
"Gracia, get up, it's light!" It's what she's for,
a messenger who tells the truth of what she sees
and slugabeds like single aunts must hear
the watcher on the heights. I like the dawn
its intellectual truth, the metaphor,
but when I wake awake, it's nearly noon.
Still and all I feel the turning around

the dewy wash of morning in the dark,
the light breaking across the haze, the sound
of robins caroling, the meadowlark,
the expectation of our final sleep
before the watcher cries, "Wake up! Wake up!"

SWEET TIME

He takes his own sweet time. His mother feels
the slow deliberation in the womb
and wishes he would come. Our anxious calls
are nothing to him, his time is not our time.
Who knows the day or who can tell the hour?
The new astrologers have read his signs
and worked out every line. His stars are sure.
But they cannot predict his plans.
We wait vainly for him to come about
but he, like any kingdom, will not come
simply because it would be best tonight.
He will arrive in his own sweet time.
His purposes are quite his own and still
astonish us to think of them at all.

POEM FOR A DAUGHTER

I shape a daughter
out of words and air

she slides from my palm
like a ripe pear

her feet are plums in my hands
she clings to me for dear life
I feel her suck
the living breath out of me
when she nuzzles me for milk

my stories are an ark
for her to sail
into groves of olives

I anchor her in tablets of stone

when she turns fourteen
red flags wave in the air

before I finish her
and get her just so
she boogies out my door
singing *let me go let me go*

ON BEING A GODMOTHER

I feel more tenderly toward helpless things
now that you are here. You teach me I am life,
that I, though barren, must be nurturing,
bending my life toward yours, to keep you safe.
When I carry you, I carry a world—
you bear the animal kingdom next to your heart,
vegetables simmer on the patchwork quilt
whose four corners you have to match just right.
Sweet cookies and crackers scatter and fall
behind us as we make a trail the birds
can follow through the snow. They twitter and call
their music as original as the first words
you lisped to name them when I bore you home
a restless seed of longings in my arms.

BAPTISM
(For Karl Theodore)

Today we wound you with the wound that heals.
Waters of chaos break over your head
and you are drowned in Christ. You bear his seal.
Only the one who raises up the dead
can bear us on that devastating flood
which saves us from ourselves and makes us whole.
We watch you coming through, our flesh and blood.
One little word shatters and kills the old.
Upon your brow and on your breast you bear
a mark that neither life nor death can change.
Your grandfather was called to put it there
with words that will forever make you strange
and alien in a world that is too grave
to risk undoing in this chaotic wave.

THE GUILD

Sweet carpenter, my little handyman,
Fiddling with every button you can find,
Quickly inspecting everything you can—
you ruin clocks to see how they unwind—
gold flies in the air like vibrant seeds,
their life amazes you, you clap your hands
and laugh. The world is filled with mysteries
which you have just begun to understand.

The schools will civilize you bit by bit,
bending your spirit to another rule,
but do not let them plunder your native wit,
which never fails to teach, a better school
than any unknown principal could build
over the years with interest in your guild.

PALACE REVOLT

The imperial two is prince about to fall,
there in his paper crown and high chair throne,
a princeling whose subjects run at his beck and call
though lately they have changed their cheerful tune,
No, they cry, like rabble in the streets,
his monarchy is overthrown for good,
the democrats surge through the palace gates,
and he must learn to gather his own wood,
to do his duty on his own. He kicks
against the pricks, the old gods take control.
Swallowing his cries like chips of granite rocks,
they know the drama has just begun to roll,
that they are overthrown and marking time
until the upstart prosecutes their crime.

STICKS AND STONES

No bravery like this, in all the world,
to match the way you arm yourself to go—
marching to meet the sun, my little girl
armed with the terrible knowledge of your foe.
I suit you up like squires their shining knights,
with provender enough to last the day,
and gleaming weapons against the power of night,
incantations to mutter, words that will slay
the terrible dragons that would hurt the least
in you, dear little girl, gone off to school,
the threatening castle of the raving beast
where unimaginable terrors rule.
The words your schoolmates fling at you like stones
can shatter your spirit, if not your armored bones.

TRIOLET FOR EMILY

Don't laugh at me she said, but people did.
Stop it, it isn't funny, said Emily.
What was that, Emily, the grownups said.
Don't laugh at me, she said, but people did.
Laugh at me one more time, I'll break your head
Emily said. She said, Don't laugh at me,
don't laugh at me, she said, and people did
stop it. Isn't it funny, said Emily.

FOR ERIK HAAKON ON HIS TENTH BIRTHDAY

Your name is filled with stories,
Kings of great and ancient glories,
Brave King Erik, noble Haakon:
Every time your name is spoken
Scepters flash and crown jewels glisten,
People bow and stop to listen.
You were named to be somebody,
Child of God, Michele and Teddy.
There is Erik, and his daughter,
Anne—we do not know her mother—
Whose great-grandson was Grandpa Haakon
Who had everybody talking
When he sat in church and whistled-
Everyone but Grandma bristled.
He was always telling stories
Like you tell of Sven and Ole.
Sunday evening, it was certain,
He would draw the parlor curtain,
Take the Rook cards out, and deal them.
Hardly anybody beat him.
Still his love, and chief endeavor,
Was that all should know their Savior.
You have much to be upholding.
Yes, your destiny is golden.
Each time you hear your great name spoken,
Remember this, dear Erik Haakon,
That many pray for you and love you.
They're watching you, with God above you.

And don't forget, our prince, and pleasure,
First of all, you are God's treasure.

STANDING ON THE PROMISES
(for Bryn Anders on his confirmation)

Today you make the promises your own—
A miracle to see you standing there
Flesh of our flesh, down to the very bone,
The words you say filling the fragrant air.
Our gallant, you stand for what is true,
Swearing your fealty to one who gave
Everything, his life and blood for you,
To give you courage, make you brave.
His word is like a sharp, two-edged sword
That kills the death within us, helps us live.
The blessings we bestow, our feeble words,
Brim at the edge of more than we can give.
Though I would press all the galaxies of good
Into the present moment, if I could.

SONG FOR RUTH AND BENJAMIN MOST HELPLESS, MOST BELOVED

Crickets are chirping in the dark and he
is come, comfort unto his mother's grief,
who, helpless, labored for him helplessly.
She's mother to his needs and his relief—
her rest is fitful as she hears him cry—
who felt him in her growing into shape
like squash. We use the garden imagery
for this. In genesis we see the grape,
ripening on the newly grafted vine,
grow heavy with the dark and purple fruit
bending again toward earth. I lift my wine
to you, mother and son, and pray you suit
each other like the cosmos and the mums
who blossom lovely as the autumn comes.

CONFIRMATION
(for Benjamin)

The bells shudder in the steeple tower
filling the air with waves of ringing sound.
Outside the church, you tremble like fresh flowers
in your new clothes, crisp under the white gowns.
The organ starts to play, the hymn begins,
you form a line and march into the church.
We raise our voices and attempt to sing,
the flashbulbs pop and sizzle, we smile and search
to find your face and somewhere in the long row
among the lilies, we see you shyly bloom
fresh as a flower. The song catches in our throats
a strange tide of mists rises in the room.
We see, as we did not, when we were young
how sweet life is, how brief its lovely song.

WORDS CROWDING THE HEART

WORDS CROWDING THE HEART

The world is insubstantial. Turning you see
the hills along the white horizon flame
and turn to darkness there beneath the sky.
You hold a piece of paper in your hand
and feel the pencil in your fingers break.
You try to find the words that are not there
you write them slowly, one by one, then look
and find they are not substantive or clear,
until, turning around you see a face.
The world is nothing, trees fall down, the hills
dissolve and there against the winter trees
a face acknowledges the hurt it feels
and hell is words crowding the heart like shades
suffering their sharp and quite substantial deeds.

POWER

Plug into me
and you will shine
like a neon sign

send requests through me
they come on
like the Holy City

I make people run
from dusk to dawn
I am the sun

touch me and live
I am charged
to give

and sing like Jesus
when the power leaves me
and hits the lady

be whole of your plague
I condescend
get off the rag

she dries up and blows away
singing my name
I do things she cannot say

at the house of the judge
I lean on death
she will not budge

I spit in her ear
lady, I need a sign
she does not hear

the sky comes on like neon
the desert buzzes around me
I stand in the tracks of a lion

POEM FOR THE TOP CHEESE

PROVOST PROVOST PROVOST PROVOST PROVOST PROVOST
PROVOSTOPROVOSTOPROVOSTOPROVOSTOPROVOSTOPROVOSTO
PROVERPESTROVERPESTOVERPESTROVERPESTPROVERTO
OVERSTEPOVERSTEPOVERSTEPOVERSTEPOVERSTEP
PRESTO PROVE PRESTO PROVE PRESTO
PRESTOPRESTOPRESTOPRESTOPRESTOP
TOPESTOPESTOPESTOPESTOPEST
STEPS TO TOP SPOT STOP
STOP STEPS TO TOPS
STOP TOP POST
STOPOSTOP
STOP
O

A FIT OF RHYMING

I'll end this foolishness: of form in time
there's much to say, but to be definite,
fancy your rhythms, playing up the rhyme.

For villanelles are silly and sublime,
too fancy, Robert Creeley would submit,
scorning this foolishness of form in time.

They toll like bells, these villanelles, they chime.
To fashion all that folly takes some wit,
some fancy rhythm. So play up the rhyme.

Dylan could do it, did it in his prime,
Ted Roethke did it once to show his grit
and beat this foolishness with form. In time

any old macho poet worth a dime
has had to write one just to show he's fit
to fancy rhythms, playing with a rhyme

winding it like a spring. And now I climb
its height proving a woman every bit
as good as they. It's foolishness. This time
I'll fancy rhythms playing up with rhyme!

PORTRAIT IN PEN AND INK

When Cady Stanton wearied of the Cause
her good friend Susan B. would quickly arrive
firm with resolve. She'd babysit the boys
and make Ms. Stanton write and theorize.
Aunt Susan bowed to no one, never slept,
her zeal consumed her. Mrs. Stanton cried
for mercy. "Susan, I'll have a baby!" It stopped
Susan, there is no record of what she said,
then she went on, making Ms. Stanton write
pages of lively prose. Her cause was just
and now we marvel at the books they wrote,
the way they spelled each other through the worst:
Susan burping the baby while she spoke,
Ms. Stanton quickly setting down their talk.

WRITING SCHOOL

The most important thing to be is free
and let your feelings pour out honestly.
The old impediments of form are dead,
as academic Robert Creeley said
while all his serious students wrote it down
so they could wear an academic cap and gown.
Their ignorance has shackled them to bliss,
their phrases strings of old cliches like this.
They risk everything twice a day in poems
and make a nuisance of themselves at home.
Original, they change from week to week,
they're all alike in that they are unique.
To hear them talk at readings one can see
they think a poet should not mean but be.
Revising is dishonest. They will say
that here some little cunning or some play
would hide the scathing truth in art. Yes, art.
Let us turn then to the educated heart,
struggling with matters of the poet's mind,
of the struggle to know the truth and not be blind.
Sing out of gentleness and love the truth.
Love it. But do not think like every youth
you can tell it. It is an art to tell.
End of this lesson. Next week, "Writing Well."

PINEVILLE

I want to go to Pineville to learn patience,
to discipline my lines, he says, to wait
and take in all the wisdom of the ancients.
He speaks, I realize his name is Kurt.
Patience. He's reading Milton now. I know
I should learn patience. He has got the time.
Midway in my life's journey I can see
there's precious little time. He says the same.
I want to go to Pineville. Smiling, I look
impatient at his time whose time is gone.
Though I can wait a day or two, my work,
no matter stern John Milton, is not done.
To wait in Pineville with my pen in hand
is right for youth, is more than I could stand.

HYPERBOLE FOR BOB STUDYING CHINESE IDEOGRAMS

He sleeps with Chinese characters
pinned up around his bed
holy as icons they bless the poems
forming in his head.

He keeps the rubrics of their shapes
falling through his dreams
he is always hewing
light from wordy beams.

He is ringed with meanings he does not
altogether know,
sometimes they come unglued
and fall on him like snow

or apple blossoms
at the end of spring
they lie like daisies
and cannot tell a thing

though there is much to tell
about this sleek scholar of art
for whom his idols fall
stung to the golden heart.

Old as an icon I smile and wonder
who worships most which beauty where
Bobby Shafto or the lady
falling for his yellow hair.

CROWN OF SONNETS: THE END OF WORDS

I

In folk songs we are bound by golden chains,
by rosy cheeks and eyes of blue. A look
transports the poorest lover to the bones.
After a glance they cannot think or talk
and seldom do. Usually they sit
in barren rooms and wish, behind closed doors,
they'd told their loves their loves. And then regret
sifts down upon them like the silent stars.
It's true. The bondage of unuttered speech
that sends riots of silly words in place
of what we really mean. But when I touch
the sweet conventions, get my truth across
I see into a world as large as God,
the awful space opening in my head.

II

The awful space opening in my head,
the place my muse inhabits all alone
as quiet as the universe inside
a stone, waiting for something or someone,
a baby bursting forth, her blossom feet
as sweet as jonquils dipped in promises
and crossed with words. Sing me a song, the lute
translates and melodies of love break forth

in dark chorales and sarabandes of words
ravel into the song, telling the truth
like any good and two-edged sword
pressing against the sinner's angry sin
cutting both ways, down into the bone.

III

Cut both ways, down into the bone,
the blood wells up, but that is all it is.
Life surges in another place. I mean
to say only what is true and press
heavily on the words and tell you more
than I can say inside of sonnet crowns,
weaving around the edge of all I dare.
I dare everything. What I want is sense
made new by pushing words into new shapes
to say what never has been said as well,
to set into a ring of words, a map
of places undiscovered. That is all.
The old explorers looked for golden lands
and found the eloquence of mythic ends.

IV

They found the eloquence of mythic ends
just as the universe was breaking down.
They comprehended starlight in the ponds,
teeming with evidence that could be seen.
Nothing meant anything beyond itself.
Words and the images of what is true
broke with the circle breaking on itself.
So I say nothing more than what I know.

We stand upon the blue pacific shore
and hear the crashing of Balboa's waves,
rolling across the vast expanses there,
feeling the turbulence within ourselves.
With nothing out there new for us to find,
we drew the circle tightly in our minds.

V

We draw the circle tightly in the mind
until it breaks. Watch out, I'll lose my head.
The world recedes. Nothing is left beyond
the old cliches, and individual words.
Broken apart, we've got to take them up
one at a time and put them back again.
Baby, I love you. Can't you ever stop.
Words, it's the words, I just can't make them mean.
I wish that I could say it better. Yes.
Decide that nothing is beyond us here
and life recedes into a bitterness.
Nothing is dreamed and nothing at the core,
a brilliance gone out of how we live
and pleasures from the words we used to love.

VI

The pleasure in the words we use for love
is gone. We've got them down to basics now.
And everything is drab. I want to live,
pushing my words farther than any do
against the rim of meaning we explore
each time that we converse. The music plays
but is it in my head or is it there

between us in the word the other says?
Speak from the heart. I know that life is short,
there's nothing we can do to make it last,
so speak a word of grace and let the hurt
be salved with comforts out of time. The past
has treasures in it, meanings I will take
to fathom mutability in talk.

VII

We fathom mutability in talk
and span the ages with a ritual word.
The conversation wandered, then you spoke.
I don't know what it was, but felt a load
of meanings, falling away like sand.
There's nothing left to say but what I know.
There's nothing I can do but give my hand
to you and say, forgive me all I do.
Death makes us gentle, as of course it should.
We know so little, what we have is gift,
the odd surprises, finding what is good
in what is common, what the gods have left:
remembrances of wonder in our bones
and songs that bind us in a golden chain.

STILL LIFE

STILL LIFE

The glass against the white shade,
the sun drawn through the water
around the stems. There is a ship
cut into the glass like ice. The sun
gleams through the glass. Outside
the branches click against the glass.
Shadows against the shade in water,
bubbles move toward the air, they glisten
around the stems, the thorns, the green
leaves pearled with dew burst
into two red roses against the white,
then open in the sun. The winter light
flowers around them, the ship of ice
sails into snow harbors. They ride
the sea of winter, cut glass ships
of ice. They carry roses, they are full
buds of red life, they are cut.
There in the sun they wait, still
life against the snow, the drab wastes.
Life, they cry, we are still life.

STUDY OF GIRL AT A WINDOW
(Oslo, October 1989)

I

The sun falls in a rectangle
on the floor. Outside the birch
trembles. September turns her head
toward darkness, trimming her yellow sails.

II

A moment ago, the sun rose
from the sea, gold in its mouth
brave as a bridegroom.

III

Bed clothes flapped like tongues
out of the rows of windows.
Ice broke up in the sound
incessantly chattering.

IV

Daffodils waited like telephones
in yellow rows
under the blue sky.

V

She was waiting for speech,
a promise.
Red peony stalks
push toward light.

VI

Words sailed her off like boats,
fragile skiffs bobbing like brown leaves
in the silver harbor.

VII

The girl standing in the window
white sheets billowing from her arms
like new sails waiting.

The birch trembles.

THE LANDLADY THE EMPIRICIST

we found it at an auction
for $5 lifted it into the Blazer
three of us groaning under the weight
and drove home bouncing up
the curb easing in toward the porch
we set it down the back wires open
and webbed by spiders there's no plug
someone said get an electrician
we struggled up the stairs heavily
setting it thud against the wall cold
and disconnected the electrician
came this morning to hook it up
does it work I asked through the screen
yes but it's old get rid of it
the wiring haven't seen one that bad
for years don't touch back there
now I'm sitting down below
writing a note to my new tenant
the stove is connected don't ever reach
behind the stove bare wires could kill you
the power spurt out like lightning
be careful I write but I'm sitting here
late at night wanting to go upstairs
and look behind the elements
to the bare wires I want to put
my finger on the open line
and see if what he says is true.

A POEM ABOUT DEATH

The sun was gold dust
sifting down and we were riding
millionaires of time
when she said look
and pitched up in the air
a man was floating in the sun
Raggedy Andy loose of joint
and I stopped the car
thinking be careful remember
this everything you see
someday it might be important
and saw the old man, a boy and another
faces raw as pie dough
and later a fat policeman
dumb as any Southern sheriff
in B grade movies
and I yelled no, no
don't move him, don't
men long accustomed to taking charge
lifted him to the chair
and I stood beside him waiting
hand to his shoulder
like one of those old tintype wedding shots
the sound fades, your honor, and I
am standing in a dim photograph, caught
in time, going brown and dusty
on someone's upright piano
the color of copper pennies and curling
I am standing on a doily in a dark parlor
married to a man with broken legs

who cannot speak
who wants someone to pay

THE RETIREMENT OF MARTIN MOHR

The lily of the valley peeps from its leaves
And fragrance swirls in the eddies of fresh air.
Spring with its boring urgency is here.
But still in all this freshness my heart grieves.
The force that gives us hope, that we believe
Moves restlessly within us, like the flower.
We flourish, then we fade, then take our leave.
But you have worked in words, and built what lasts.
Young lovers, wandering through the halls of sleep,
Remember words you taught them, and sing your praise
Into their lover's ear. They hear the past
Speaking its music to them as you speak
And give them means to mark their novel ways.

MIDSUMMER'S EVE

Now when the haze is settling in the glen
and light falls softly through the maple trees
the meadow breathes its secret history.
The gravestones find their tongues. Gentlemen
and ladies dance in the summer fields again,
their presences are large and filled with glee.
Come, they call us from our reverie,
dancing us lightly over the heavy stones.
Earth moves beneath our feet. Over the mist
the stars come out like distant farms
lit by the candles of the sabbath meal.
All the company of heaven takes its rest.
Silently moving in each others' arms,
we hear the light, celestial bodies reel.

ELISABETH KOREN WRITES
Strawberries: June 1854

Strawberries. Soon there will be strawberries.
Strawberries not to have you here with me.
Without you I can only write: it is
spring, it will soon be summer blossoms, free
for you, for me as we turn the evening out,
the meadow coming green out of the blue.
If you were here, we'd walk the spring about
strawberry blossoms. I would gather you,
the sun dying against the western hills.
Without you here I have to write my love,
pressing against the letter where it kills.
Love, I keep writing you a little of
my love, blossoms, strawberries, this I know,
dead letters, strawberries, how they grow.

ELISABETH KOREN
(Letter to Linka Preus, in Wisconsin: July 1856)

They loaded up the wagons
and left without me.
It was too hot to take the babies.
The heat is terrible.
I long for salt.

The baby is gnawing on a bone,
the girl has named mosquitoes
a funny name.

The roses are out.
I've found a bird
named cowbird.
Do you know it?

Outside in the humid dawn
a meadowlark sings like rain.
I long for you like salt.

Koren is gone this month.
I wish I'd come with.
The rain sweeps in
across the prairie.
I'll write this letter
and take pleasure
in the feel of words
coming to shape in my hands.

The rain comes down hard
like applause in the garden.

The baby is fussing.
I go to pick him up.
Talk to me, I say, talk.
Goo, he trills
sucking the bone dry
of its salt.

A THEORY OF FICTION

it is 1933
on a Minnesota farm
we hear the wind, the dust
seeps through the windows
we are breathing through wet rags
the evening sun is a great red ball

I go to study
The Odyssey
where heroes lie around
drinking wine and listening
to a blind poet sing

now in the idyllic dust
I see a lady in a long dress
walking in a photograph
along the edge of a lake
everything is brown and white

she is singing ballads
music from her guitar
washes the trees with light

sunset and evening star

ODE ON AN ENGLISH TEACHER
(for Anne Pederson's 80th birthday)

The harvest days are come, the russet hues
of autumn, fiery maples, burnished oaks
blossom around her. When she speaks she knows
the seasons, spring and fall; I see her look
across the years at me and when she talks
I hear the ripeness in her flawless speech
the syntax of precision I would teach.

At moments she could level me with words,
with sentences that I would die to keep—
she read the speech of Clytemnestra's guard
spying the fires of victory lighting up
better than any actor in the slips—
she takes her glasses off and peers across
the printed page and gives us Aeschylus.

At Christmas she would read the poetry
of Eliot and Shakespeare. "Set down this,"
she read precisely, letting the imagery
live like the Nightingale. Today we praise
the balance of her language, phrase on phrase
a world as big as Eden which she built
in all the little gardens where we dwelt.

Once in a farm museum we walked past
a fan for winnowing the harvest grain.
She stopped and thought back to her farmgirl days
saying, "I see the chaff against the sun
the grain falling beneath it, ripe and clean.

It makes one think of judgment, doesn't it,
Jesus dividing the nations, right and left?"

She gave us memory, the civil world
of Dante, Austen, Dickinson and Yeats
and we were changed. The patterns hold,
we carry on, the knowledge in our hearts
that love is ultimate, believing first
against the old confusions of the flesh
warring against itself, the ancient clash.

The autumn flames and blazes once again
and we are come to celebrate her years.
Once she preached to us of Simeon
holding the baby Jesus in his arms,
her gestures mimicked his, she held him there,
a woman bearing Christ before our eyes
ripe with the Word that changed and made her wise.

HOMECOMING
(Elegy for Gerda Mortenson, Dean of Women, Augsburg College, 1923-1963)

It is the big Homecoming festival on high
and she is ordering all the saints
and seraphim around the glassy sea.
While angels make ambrosia by the pints,
Michael is dusting out his favorite haunts.
The golden streets are bright and shiny clean
polished by cherubs to a brilliant sheen.

She will be checking out the angels' work
while going over all the lists of guests.
Nothing escapes her keen and careful look.
The tables groan with milk and honey blest
and crystal bowls of water. Life at last,
at last, she will cry, at last, bustling to greet
the honored guests parading heaven's streets.

The choir sings "Washed in the Lamb's pure blood."
General Booth beats time on his big bass drum.
Our voices ring with laughter. This is good.
Ambrosia for the guests, peaches and cream.
Look at her standing there at God's right arm.
The golden windows of eternity
dazzle and make it difficult to see.

The feast goes on. She introduces us
to all the saints, greeting them one by one.
Our grandmother is singing with the choirs
beside Luther and Saint Augustine.

We walk the gallant walks of heaven's green.
But down below the snows of winter fall.
The grief we felt hammered us like a bell.

For something ended for us when she died.
She was the solid rock for us and more.
A woman planting crocus when she heard,
said, "No, oh, Gerda is not dead. I hear
the celebrations going on for her.
Homecomings, grand reunions are her style.
She is all motion on a turning wheel."

She brings us to the King and to the Son
to meet and mingle with in social joys
with saints in white before the shining throne,
a foretaste we have had at Gerda's teas.
The party is not long and yet is days.
We walk beside the crystal stream that flows
over our tears and every human woe.

The sapphires and the rubies dance and shine.
Portals of pearl shimmer all through the house.
The river glows beside us. We drink wine
and keep our revels with amazing grace,
beneath the many fruited tree of peace,
raising our glasses while she makes the toast
to God, the Lord, the Bride, the guest and host.

DREAM

She was in a brown photograph
in an apron and long dress.
Horses were hitched to a rake,
wheat fields lay in shocks around her.

The brown hills arched
against the dusty light
and the river was the shape of silence.
She was propped against the stubble

watching the morning sun
in the cut fields beside her.
The fragrance of dawn
rose from the heavy dew.

She saw his yellow hat
moving through the green fields.
He walked into the blue water
and stood in the sparkling stream.

Larks flitted in the meadow,
the sun flared behind him.
He was reaching from his sphere
into the flat spaces where she lay.

She felt something hitch and press.
It pushed against the level plain
like rough and stubby fingers
moving to undo her frame.

THE BOND OF STONE
for Catherine and Henry Horn

Husband, my flesh, body I know as mine
familiar as a clam, predictable
as English weather, foggy mist and rain
followed by periods of clearing, I will
love you, I promised, my sentiments were full
dear stranger at my side, still unexplored
a hidden country whose darknesses I bear.

Here on my hand I wear a stone of light
dug from a vein of diamond in the earth,
your signet on the treaty we have kept
for years, the careful border of the north
disarmed but bravely watched. The restless south
more troublesome, encamped with stricter guards
who could not stem the river with their swords.

This noon beside you in the winter sun
turning the rock to watch the light play
and shimmer on my hand, I lost the stone—
fallen into the darkness of memory
where I had set it like my jewelry.
The stone is like an old museum piece
holding in fire our mutual histories.

We are lost, I think, searching for the stone.
Each crystal of ice a likely diamond
turning to water, into droplets of sun
as I lift them toward me in my trembling hand.

I know the truth of water, our Christian bond,
but want the stone, its hard reality,
the thing between us a mineral surety.

After noon, you drift into sleep, I fret
hard after that stone turning things upside down.
Your breathing falls and rises, your great heart beats,
while you trudge the dark and misty lands.
It's then I think to open up the blinds
to see more clearly in the winter sun—
whether the light will flare inside the stone.

It catches the light, the diamond comes alive
beside you, like fire on a distant hill
flaring with news of your return. Go brave,
my love, beside me as the darkness falls.
The dusk is gathering round us deep and still,
I hold the light binding us, round and round.
Come, turn slowly toward me, love, my bond.

THE INHERITANCE

You have come back to silence, to this place
as quiet as a ticking clock—a swinging door,
a creaking gate, the wind sighing through trees
and then the quarter chimes. The morning chores
are quickly done. Once pails clanked and the milk
would fall into the separator pan,
the steam rising above its churning bulk.
But here you are back to silence once again—
you've built a house where you can make retreat
against the hurly burly of the world,
just like your home. Listen! the barnyard gate
slams in the grueling wind. A little girl
speaks to her father. Then the silence grows.
it fills the morning and the spent hay mows.

GOING HOME

The February fields stretch into haze.
She sees that all the icehouses are down
except for one and notices the size
of every farm and every little town
along the way. She measures time by change,
remembering the road by Model T,
by train, remarking on the new or strange,
the rich mosaic of the winter trees.

At Glenwood, when we reach the lookout hill
and see full fourteen miles across the lake
she says, I like this view. I ask how she feels.
That afternoon when I am driving back
I see a pickup on the slushy ice.
The waves will overcome us. Don't think twice.

FINDING THE GRAVE OF KAREN NEUBERG LARSEN 1833-1871, DECORAH, IOWA

Here in the growing darkness we find her tomb
inside an overgrown bank of trees.
Her children lie around her, stone on stone,
and to her left his second helpmeet lies.
Last night we read the story of her death,
the myrtle greens they wove into a cross
to cover her with flowers in a wreath.
We saw her children give her one last kiss.
The light fading as we walk about,
the children do not like our graveyard stroll
and rightly sense a chill inside the heat,
but we are more familiar with the pall
of darkness there below. Our words are bonds,
a blessed country, like a stone of friends.

ELEGY FOR A CHRISTIAN LADY

It is not simply that a lady died.
The levels of the universe are gone
beside her. Here a Christian lady lies
set in the ceremony none can learn.
Heaven is spinning in her hazel eyes,
she enters in the pearly gates of horn
and we have lost an old connection with
the storied world of horse and buggy myth.

On Sundays she could play a Crosby hymn
or Bach toccata at the local church,
for dinner she would fix a stewing hen
she'd killed and pick some roses by the porch
to decorate the table where she spun
the family yarns. Now her remains are words
that we cannot remember as we might
as she is folded into marble light.

On busy afternoons she'd climb into
the carriage, ride to ladies aid or choir,
leaving behind the chores still left to do.
She took her pleasures in the changing hours,
the isinglass in winter dusk she knew,
the seasons of the flowers and their cures.
The ceremonies of the years she kept
in style. Her way with loveliness was apt.

She knew that dying had its purposes:
the mysteries of animals we set
our teeth into for life, of milk and cheese,

of picking eggs from chickens in their nests
and how to fasten ties in homemade quilts:
we praise her though we little need the skill
that mutely rests inside her placid skull.

She practiced what is lovely with her hands
and saw, as we cannot, how beauty lives.
Beside the roses and the hens she stands
for what is good and true. The earth receives
her as she is and knows her as a friend.
As we who gather round her take our leave
we stand here dumbly wondering what we know
and at the lovely place she has to go.

POULTER'S MEASURES FOR PETRINA

Her breasts flopped down her chest
as Norway hangs from Sweden—
when she walked she carried the country
off with her in the Eden

of her arms—she was Christmas, Easter,
spring and Syttendemai.
We laughed to see Petrina laugh,
we never saw her cry.

At Christmas we heard her
squealing like a sow
and hurried down the long hall
to see Petrina's row.

Her fat hand held a marsipan
Christmas pig whose head
she'd just bit off—a red ribbon
bled from the body. She said

that eating it reminded her
of the farm—she was merely
imitating the sounds pigs made
when they'd slaughtered them yearly.

And when she spoke of death,
though she seldom did, she'd snort
the same words farmers used for stock:
"Eg driver å rottne bort!"

Settlers used the same phrase
to tell of hogs drowned
in spring floods to rot away
until their flesh was found

by farm girls herding goats
back home in the mountains,
pork carcasses plump with rot,
insides all worm eaten.

Petrina knit all day
singing lullabies,
and told of babies she'd rocked to sleep—
when they heard her voice, their cries

stopped. Her song was the wind
moaning through the slats
of houses by the sea, the music
had no sharps or flats,

but keened between the ledges
of the twelve tone scale.
Petrina was all fat and sound,
nothing about her was frail.

And so she sang all day,
knitting profuse skeins
of unpremeditated art
despite her nagging chilblains

and standing up to adjust
her breasts with her generous arms
would laugh, "Nei, eg rottne bort!"
—I rot like a pig on a farm.

Her blithe spirit made us happy
while we worked, her uncommon girth,
her songs, her laughter and her language,
common as country earth.

LEGACY

THE CHRISTIAN RELIGION IS THE MOST PHYSICAL OF RELIGIONS

As we are singing hymns of Jesus' love,
she puts her hand around her husband's arm
crooking it slightly into the gentle groove
it makes against his side. Her hand is firm,
I like the strong blue vessels standing out
against her bony knuckles. I like her touch,
the way she turns her head to hear the text,
the sharp amen she sighs into the church,
the way she looks when Jesus tells the twelve
they must not love their wife or husband more
than they love him, they'll never find themselves
until they lose themselves. And that is sure.
Christ moves in every neighbor's Sunday clothes
the lilting way she moves him with her pose.

COMPELLED, THEY WRITE

Jerome burst into tears, like Augustine
was shaken into writing books. He wrote
thousands of pages, parchment, one by one,
trying to understand the fall of Rome,
northern barbarians tippling in the streets.
The Eternal City taken, they wrote books
against the end of time. Writers write.
They never say, if I had time. It seeks
them out, they cry, O let me sleep. Their muse
stands like a flaming angel over them.
Falling asleep, they hear a deathless phrase
buzz in their ears like a saw. Asleep
they dream of words and wake. Compelled, they write
against the end of time, against the night.

LEGACY

I

The plant your mother gave you bloomed last
    night
you say, deftly removing one dry leaf.
Your mother kept it in the rich estate
she left for you, knowing you'd keep it safe.
The petals flame in your hand. I feel you long
for her, the summer in the lilac trees,
and watch her as you handle lovely things,
a legacy that lives in you these days.

There's nothing for this sorrow. Every year
she went to decorate her mother's grave
with flowers, rituals for you to share.
And now you keep them, knowing how we live.
The ease we have with nature has an end,
I mark it when you hold the flower stem.

II

Sometimes when we are riding in the sun,
time stops, the afternoon becomes a way
to celebrate the hours, the pitch of one
against another. Day after day
we lose the splendor, find it there again
radiant and timeless. Sent to us, it comes
just as the horses make their delicate turn
against the sun. Our chariot dips and climbs

gone like Elijah into the heart of God
where no festivities are ever done
and light is fundamental. On we ride,
beyond the gray horizon, in the sun
laughing like Christians in the face of death,
the enemy we fathom out of our depths.

III

The monks who wrote of love were celibate,
they fled the world of women and the flesh
but love they could not flee, the desolate
and empty spaces of the heart made ash
by visions of their love, complete and whole.
They dreamt of love that no one ever finds.
Only in heaven, love will never fail,
it was like dying making love their end.

The world is still before us, fresh and green.
That old fool spring is lying in our bones
though autumn hunkers deep inside the seed
as ordinary as an office phone
ringing against our flesh, against our loves.
We perish sweetly, walking toward our graves.

MAGDALA

Look, he said, she is not thinking of the poor,
wasting that precious oil like it was free,
and then, wiping his feet dry with her hair.
Wastrel, think of the starving she could feed,
said Judas as he counted up the cost,
visions of silver clinking in his head.
He knew the price of bread and wine at most,
but oil, that was a price beyond his ken.
Her deed, extravagant and beautiful,
shocked the religious. Here, my Lord, my God,
she bathed his dirty feet with precious oil.
It was the least that I could do, she said,
He gave me life, I was the poorest poor,
she said, wiping his feet with her fragrant hair.

SONNET FOR GOOD FRIDAY

The man is beaten on the cheeks and nose.
His beard is cleft, his hair hangs in a long braid.
Nine hours ago they nailed him to the cross
and where the nails pierced him, his body bled.
But he is dead. The fruit of Eden's tree.
he hangs between the heavens and the earth,
alone and set apart. He made a cry
tasting the thirst from deep inside his mouth.
There is no word but babble from the crowd.
The cross drives like a nail through the skull
and we are silent. Who can utter words
against those mocking cries, the pitiless nails?
The scene bears down, deep, deep inside the bone
like nails pounded into this only son.

MATINS

Two cardinals against the snow
on dark branches over the white
snow, against the blue heavens
singing on the branches, their chapel.
The red cardinals gather
in the sun. The blue caves in,
it rims around the cardinals
against the snow, suited up
for Sunday, they whistle
like rude boys, out of the blue.
They sing glory be, glory be,
the morning sun.

AMBROSE
WHOSE SYMBOL IS A BEEHIVE

I suck like a bee
at Ambrose' lips
a foot of honey
in little sips

and buzz it home
to the busy hive
a honeycomb
in the deep archive

where scholars come
to taste the sweet
and then grow dumb
with what they eat

KATYDID

Katydid, katydid, singing
at my window, are you
tired of your song? I am
almost asleep. You screech
how green I am, how green
I am. Katydid
leaves of grass, I am
singing katydid, katydid
at my window how green
I am leaves of grass.

DAME WISDOM IN LOVE

In love, our cook, Dame Wisdom, is in love—
she lights the candles for the Sabbath meal,
dancing around the table from the stove
with dishes to make the stoniest palate reel.
The wines sparkle, but, oh, my friends her eyes
laugh like the heavens on a moonless night
when far into the dense and lavish skies
the Milky Way scatters her robe of light
grandly across the meadows of the dark
where Wisdom and her witty love can play
like children in a grand celestial park,
lost to the wheeling planets, night and day,
feeding on apples, drinking flagons of wine,
on a bed of spices, there Dame Wisdom dines.

SHEBA

The Queen of Sheba rides in a great train,
her camels laden with gold, hitch and lurch
across the desert toward King Solomon—
who watches from his gold and marble porch.
The king's men take out their trumpets to play
the grand processional: The Queen is here.
Her embassy of curiosity
shimmers with heat in the pomegranate air.
Solomon gives the Queen the best he has,
wisdom that spends its genius for her sake,
she curls up beside him, sugar and spice,
she whispers, how much money do you make?
Enough for two, he smiles, fingering her gold,
the key changes, his love runs hot and cold.

THEA RØNNING, MISSIONARY TO CHINA (1865-1899) SISTER OF MISSIONARY HALVOR, AND N.N., THE BOY FROM TELEMARK

I

(Bø i Telemark, 1887)

The dull sound of an axe thuds through the trees,
a young woman looks back and boards the train
leaving behind her home and family.
The hills rise in a mist of Norway pine
up to the mountains, where, stone upon stone,
her fathers cleared a farm and grew their food
beside the stubborn rock and scenic wood.

Was China roaring in her head as loud
as God the day she pledged herself anew
before the congregation? Where did she read
of Hudson Taylor and his mission to
the teeming millions of China? There's not a clue
in any archive, or any brittle page
crumbling with news for this eavesdropping age.

II

(Bø i Telemark, 1985)

A scholar found some letters in a drawer
worn with constant reading, and then tied up
in careful bundles, no one knew what for.
She was a dead surprise, though we had maps
which I had pored over. Her brother's lips
dripped with a honey I was wild to taste,
the stories of my own, but distant place,

the legends of our people in the hills
of Norway; he never mentioned Thea once.
I read our history in his published tales,
the robber printed in our common genes
who fled Denmark and the Danish prince,
the priest whose Protestant convictions fought
the pagan revelries of girls and goats.

III

(Arendahl Church, near Peterson, Minnesota,
    June 1890)

Now she is standing in an country church
in a field in Fillmore Country, praying to go
to China in a year. She wants to preach,
she feels the Spirit in her, the words flow,
It is like Pentecost again, to know
that God can use her gifts. A bit surprised,
Thea's mouth fills with a tongue of fire.

"Women," a pastor mutters, "should not speak
in church or public meetings, read St. Paul."
But the words flow out, Sister Thea starts to preach,
a sweet fulfillment of the prophet Joel.
Her vision reaches all around the world:
she sees her mother working in a mountain hut,
and Chinese women living on river boats.

"Dry bones," she cries, "God will make these dry bones rise,
it is the living God who speaks today.
'Go, my children,' is what the Savior says,
'Go, preach the Gospel here and far away.'"
The Spirit shakes them and takes their breath away.
They peer across the wealthy fields of June
and see them ripen in the eschaton.

Silence. The congregation shuffles and weeps,
and older pastor loudly clears his throat.
In the back a big farmer stands up,
and speaks, over the crowds of woolen coats,
"I guess if Sister Rønning is willing to go,
that each of us could give a little more.
I pledge $50 every year."

She and Halvor could be sent. They rode
the prairie asking pioneers to give
enough to keep them solvent. By spring they had
rumbled down thousands of country roads and drives
speaking to every Haugianer alive
about their call to China. Late that fall
they left the stubbly fields of Arendahl.

IV

(Christmas 1891, Hankow, China)

Her first letter home was filled with some disquiet,
the weather was cold and sanitation bad,
odors of death and waste reeked in the streets.
She fell sick and could not leave her bed,
but could not rest with all of China's need
keening outside the compound. Soon she will speak
Chinese to the women once a week.

She grew to love the peaches in their bud,
the mulberry, and making of raw silk,
she wrote hundreds of letters to ladies aids
at home asking them for homemade quilts
to give the Chinese women, money to build
a school for orphans, especially for the girls
who were abandoned to the Christian schools.

V

(Fan'cheng, China, 1895)

In four years she knew the language well
and visited the women in their homes.
She loved the tea, the ancient rituals
of China, but feared that civil wars would come.
In 1893, it came to them,
they fled. And then returned. The fields are white
to harvest, please send more help, she wrote.

Himles and Landahl arrived. Thea went
to meet them. She traveled down the Han River
eager to meet the ones who had been sent.
Bandits marauded the countryside, terror
stalked them. Thea sailed the boat-filled water.
When she arrived in Hankow she went to stay
with Daniel Nelsons, the first from Iowa.

She met them there, Carl Landahl, a single man
who heard the call to China and came with those
the China mission had sent out. On their return
robbers set upon them, taking their clothes
and everything. Thea took all these woes
in good humor, staying in bed until they found
some garments which her hostess had to mend.

She fell in love. Landahl was tall and thin,
and bore himself proudly. They planned to move
some miles further north to Taipingti'en
to found a mission. Their work went well, they lived
for others, Thea's health was much improved.
Their work with women flourished, Thea wrote
"Their need to hear of Jesus breaks my heart."

In March of 1898 they came
to Hankow for the Annual Conference
of their little mission, Thea told them
how she took advantage of each chance
she found to speak to women at least once
of Jesus and their need to study with fervor.
That night she fell sick with a high fever.

VI

(April 1898, Fairibault, Minnesota)

The missionary papers printed up
a special page with black lines all around
a cross and Thea's photo. A bitter cup
for the struggling mission. It stung her friends
to see the gravestone in a foreign land.
The Chinese dressed her in a robe of silk,
ivory as the cream skimmed off fresh milk.

I read those pages in the magazine
as though I am boning up on recent news.
Turning that page to focus on the scene
where she is dead, I know that I will lose
a treasure I have gained, but did not choose.
She was so small and yet her life had grown
bigger than all the legends she had known.

Her brother left this tale for me to write,
perhaps he could not see, for bitter tears,
the legendary places of her heart.
Or thought more of his literary heirs
than of the legacy of her short years.
He published all his losses in the books
I read in dusty attics where I look

diligently for the myths I have been told
to keep. They crumble to pieces in my hands,
the dusty legacy of all these old.
She disappears like houses made of sand.

It's only telling stories that will mend
this loss I feel as keen as those who stood
beside her casket speaking of her faith in God.

SWEETNESS AND LIGHT AT CANTERBURY

She says, lifting her rucksack, Let it fall
to ruin, all this decorated stone.
People are starving, let the wind and rain
make rubble of it. Over her head, the heel
of Jesus presses down and colors fill
the darkness where she stands. The morning sun
flares through the leaded glass where stories burn
in rainbows around the drab and earnest girl
beatified among these mendicants.
Bolingbroke rattles off his guilty prayers,
Beckett is murdered at a bloody mass,
the Wife of Bath contributes a shiny pence.
Rude hawkers hawk their cheap and pious wares
while sinners feed themselves by staining glass.

FORTUNATUS AT FOREST LAKE
A POEM OF THE TRUE CROSS

I

He saw the Royal Banners wave in the sun
as pilgrims in a grand procession bore
a splinter of the True Cross for the Queen
to set inside her abbey. The sun flared
on the silver casket and the gold they wore,
he saw light flashing, yellow daffodils
and heard his music in the abbey halls.

His sun drenched vision took no thought of us
standing beneath the cross in Forest Lake
keeping a vigil after all these years.
The cross looms in the darkness, light on dark,
rising above us from Hosanna's rock.
Over us heaven wheels, we see Orion
and then we sing a quiet song of Zion.

II

The shovels clang against the stony ice.
We set the alleluia in the ground
and then our song goes silent. We have dressed
ourselves against the darkness and our end
knowing there's nothing permanent. We stand
helpless against the ravages of time,
against the dark confession in a rhyme:

Ashes, ashes, all fall down. We cry
against the death of light within our hearts.
Then, suddenly, we see it shine, we see
water like sunlight flaming in the street
changed to St. John's Apocalpyse of light.
The fire speaks before us like a tongue
caroling through us, breaking into song.

III

Take the oak tree, hew it into beams
and make a cross, burning the leaves to dust.
Now let the fire purge us with its flame
flaring like petals come at Pentecost.
And, like the royal banners, set us fast
against the wooden beams on which no leaves
will sprout again, the death in which God lives.

Remembrances of leaves gone up in smoke.
Inscribe my death upon my ashen brow
and mark me with the cross you made of oak.
So let my bones rejoice, my God, in you,
whose mercies dwell like water in the snow.
O keep me in the covenant of light
and crucify my sin. O send me life!

JINGLE JANGLE

Doodle me simple
doodle me bugs
doodle me jangle
cutting up rugs

say I have given
the good poems away
flung them so freely
away away

say I have gone now
to jingle dark coins
to dicker for rugs
where the delta joins

the sea, O say I have gone
to find a new song
rich with adagios
bluesy and strong.

A REVELRY OF HARVEST

NO RELIGIOUS VERSE
("Strongly encouraged topics: positivity, recovery and nature. No hateful, overly religious or vulgar poetry.")

Wisdom today is secrets told, revealed.
The pious verities from ancient books
Are outworn dogmas, mysteries long sealed
Tightly behind a tomb of unmoved rocks
Which we have left our intellects to guard
So nothing out of nature will break loose
And wreck the faith we have in our own lords.
Breaking a silence saves us, breaking a truce
Frees us from human bondage, life never ends,
We spiral into finitudes of time,
Our fundamental enemy, make friends
With vegetable signs, creeds more sublime
Than Jesus nailed to a bloody cross
Than God becoming flesh to die for us.

LAKE VALAMO, FINLAND

If they were to make a jewel of you
It would be made with water pressed from the lake
at Valamo, clear enough to take
Into a glass and drink, like morning dew.
Pressed down against the sea you would come through
sparkling, as clear as diamond, washed in the wake
of water a vintage the monks could never make.
Your soul trills like a brook, bubbling, new.
The sun strikes the water. It takes the fire.
All the elements we need to live
Come daily to us in the smallest things.
It is a simple grace that can inspire
A heart of darkness to catch light and give
Out of its plenty, and take on airy wings.

DAEDALUS

Riding like Daedalus above the clouds,
over the smoky bay of Reykjavik,
filled with the finest foods, I feel like God,
nothing below me is worth a second look.
If you can see them, cars are like tiny dots,
houses the size of words on a little page.
Riding above the square and distant spots
It is easy to dismiss this terrible age.
But nothing I can do will change the tears
falling in the heart of one who weeps.
I ride above the slow and turning years
dreaming as one whose weakened conscience sleeps:
Fooled by the distance from the human heart
Where riding high deceives from the very start.

RECOLLECTION

They come again, those feelings: a melody,
Quietly picked out recalls them now
On the instrument of memory.
One note after another, and somehow
Transported across the miles, memory flies,
The senses feel almost as if we're there,
And we are walking down the hill, the sky
Is always blue, the meadows, if they were,
Swaying with flowers, early summer days
Behind us on the album of the mind.
Yes, I remember them, one always does,
But did they happen, whispers the summer wind?
I think they did, the music has me say,
The melody, the notes I've come to play.

THE TURNING PAGE

The world of memory is round with words.
A word splashes like a stone in a quiet pool.
The rings echo in the water, according to rule,
And keep on rolling, regular and undisturbed.
Then, an old wave barely there is heard
And everything that was is out of school,
As sharp as it has ever been. I'm no one's fool
But see those children there, playing cards.
They've been in half the towns of Europe, seen
It all, and know more than any kids their age.
They will forget their insouciance and pride
And think, much later, of where they have been,
And watch relentlessly the turning page
Of history, and marvel how quick the ride.

GIRL WEEPING

The night is full of voices: Laughter falls
Into the quiet waters where the sound breaks.
Then all is silence. A bed above me creaks.
Off in the distance someone coughs. In the hall
Fluorescent lights buzz like an urgent call.
Something has broken without a sound. I wake
And hear the silence in the next room ache.
Nothing can be done for it, nothing at all.
Perhaps some ancient grief made sharp again
By some rough stone waiting within the heart
To hone the blade keener than it had been
Ages ago when first it cut and hurt.
The past opens within us like a wound
That cannot fathom this deep and wordless sound.

THE KEYSTONE; STAVANGER CATHEDRAL

The keystone in the arch, it is the one
That holds it all together, all the weight
Of all the many feet of ancient stone,
It bears the whole cathedral, its granite state,
And when you look at it you do not think
How dangerous, how very brave of them
To trust this little piece of stone, to link
These lofty heights of rock that hulk and loom
Over the city to gravity, the force
We cannot overcome without the work
Of rocket scientists, who as they course
The lofts of physics now are turning back
To say that something far beyond us made
Everything that is, that has, or can be said.

THE ELEMENT OF STONE

This rock that only dynamite can shear
From its dark hold, shattering and bursting apart,
Is strong enough to hold a house, to bear
Whatever is set upon it, it comes from the heart
Of stone, the cauldron of molten fire that seethes
Deep in the core of earth, though when it cools
Cannot be moved, except by the steel teeth
Engineers from lithographic schools
Hammer into it when they try to build
Roads or houses into the troll-like back
Of the hulking rock. The imagery is filled
With confidence, the faith alone in fact
That we can set our houses into the stone
And gravely trust in gravity alone.

THE COMPOSER OF THE WORLD
(For Nils Henrik Asheim)

He makes music out of air and things,
And time, the fourth dimension we must have
For sound. He hears what is around him sing.
All earth, and heaven, too, plays what he loves,
He takes it from the ordinary day
And sets it in a form that we can hear
The horns, the bells, the metal pipes, they play
Music that only he has heard before
But now we hear it in the rainy night
As he is beating time against the dark
Bringing the quiet misty air to light
Teaching us all to hear again, to mark
That harmony that once composed the spheres
Singing its new song in our stone deaf ears.

A REVELRY OF HARVEST

If you look more closely, the church nestled behind
The grove of trees over there in the golden field,
You see that it is left abandoned, the blind
Windows, shuttered over, the doors are nailed
Shut, the steeple blunted, and no bell rings.
Around the back, a row of graves like teeth
Protrude from the prairie where a meadowlark sings—
Its mournful song rises above the heath,
An elegiac sound marking the end
Of something that will never quite be gone:
A settlement of martyrs to the wind
And rain, now waiting gravely in their bones
For Christ to waken them with trumpets, horns,
A revelry of harvest in these fields of corn.

SHOPPING FOR SHOES WITH MY FATHER

His foot, incapable of subtle moves,
Thrusts itself forward into the shoe I push
Over his toes, around his heel. He shoves
His instep into the arch. The blood rushes
To my head as I bend down to tie the knot,
I feel him fading into his parchment skin.
He used to stand above me, dressing me up
school mornings, unraveling the tangled skein
My garter belt had fallen into overnight.
He is whistling softly, the garters click
In the sleepy dark. Outside the winter light
Is breaking over the prairie sky, the clock ticks
In the hall downstairs, bringing me to school—
And this, the way it works, the Golden Rule.

PARISH DUTIES

The dailiness of life, the dishes, clothes,
The dusting, sweeping up of little deaths—
Legions of little things under my nose
Perishing—all while I set my pearly teeth
Into the cereal which guarantees
A longer life. More cooking, picking up.
My mother spent her afternoon at teas,
At Ladies Aides, and circles, filling her cup.
She entertained them, made them laugh and cry
Telling her stories gleaned from the parish store.
Rustling like flowers in their fancy dress, they'd dry
Their tears and leave for home. Then as before
Take up the laundry, put the kettle on,
Musing at how they'd laughed, and things got done.

WEDDING IN AUTUMN
for Blake and Katie

Nature has bloomed for you, its gaudy end
Lavishing bright colors on the town,
As if to celebrate your day and send
Bountiful and ample banners round,
Strewing your way, like roses in the spring.
Though we know autumn, and November's chill,
To hear you swear your love, exchange your rings,
Is like an April day, with daffodils
Lining the garden, bending to bless you both.
Great congregations of them turn and bow
As all creation does, taking the cloth
To give your ceremony favor now.
Flesh and bone has nothing better to say
Than you your promises this wedding day.

GRIEF IN THE DEAD OF WINTER

It feels like grief, but life goes by quickly,
Hardly without a second thought. The hours
Slip by, the rhythms of the normal day
Fill each moment with tasks, we think the cares
Consuming us will soon be done and over,
And then we will be free, have time to live,
But then, in the kitchen, as we reach to cover
The lettuce, shake the water from the leaves,
Watching the water pearl off the delicate green,
Life seems a stretch of loss and change. We age,
Our parents die, the children leave, we speed
Toward an end we fear, against which we may rage,
The lettuce in the crisper spoils and rots
As we are nosing out the family plot.

ELEGY FOR T. ROBERT BURNTVEDT
for Laverne
(24 December 1996)

A word will not return him, nor dispel
The hurt that you are feeling: he is gone.
The tears come freely, drawn from a salty well
That feeds the pool of sorrow in the stone.
Against this enemy, who is no friend,
His heart and flesh could not prevail. He lost
The final battle, sheer will could not contend
Against the prince of darkness, though the cost
Of that defeat did not incur a debt—
Except for love, which he is paying now
To his Redeemer. Do not, my friend, forget
He lost the skirmish, not the final bout.
Death has betrayed your love. The only word
Will wipe away your tears is Christ our Lord.

ROOT VEGETABLES

Root vegetables, the ones that hide in the
   ground
Grow in the sandy soil in the north.
Rutabagas, parsnips, carrots, the brown
And yellow small potatoes, cling to the earth,
Wait for the gardener's summer stewardship.
Wresting them from the ground, shaking the soil
From them, washing and storing them under the steps
Where they will wait, fruits of the sunshine's toil
Until the dark midwinter settles in
And one by one they will be taken up
Into the kitchen where the pale sun
Fades in the early afternoon. The soup
Fragrantly simmers and here in my hand I hold
A small green leaf sprouting against the cold.

SONG WITHOUT NOTES

The silence she inhabits like a room
Follows her through each day. She cannot hear
The door open, the boiling kettle scream,
The faucet running. The hardest thing to bear:
She cannot hear the music, or bend her voice
To sing in harmony, or by herself.
On Sunday evenings she would sing for us
Taking her mother's music down from the shelf
To sing "Forgotten" and "Jerusalem."
She tuned the architecture of our hearts
With song. Already we ache for evening hymns
Filling the house with peace, her quiet art
Using the rest—to which she now belongs—
To touch the rim of heaven with her song.

MY BRILLIANT CAREER

We always write about it, worry it
To death: if I should die before my work,
My brilliant work, is written down, and left
Immortal on a shelf of deathless books,
How terribly impoverished the world
Will be, for I have things to say, great truths
As clear as water, valuable as gold,
That I must chisel into stone, hard proofs
Of my existence, only I can give,
A stone confessional of careless deeds
Scattered about the city where I live,
Coming up thistles, tares and weeds:
A lithographic record, mine alone,
Something that will not perish, blunt as stone.

FRAGMENTS OF MY FATHER

"I'm having metaphors," my father says
Looking off center toward the birds flying
Over my head, beyond the synapses.
His brain, the books all say, is slowly dying,
But suddenly he sees what must be done.
Bending his knees to dust the rocking chair
Memory breaks in his head like a shaft of sun,
"Each time I kneel to dust I say a prayer
For one of you." Our Lord and Savior said
Call no man good, and I agree that all
Have sinned, but now that the cells inside his head
Scramble his thoughts, torment his generous soul,
I hate the metaphors, the gathered birds,
My own vocation tangling a good man's words.

FLESH AND BLOOD

He ministers unto his flesh and blood,
It happens every evening when I wash
My father, and settle him in his narrow bed,
After the benediction of the flesh
He shares with Mother. I soap and wash him clean,
He walks into her room to say good night,
To say a Bible verse, to pray, to lean
Toward her and kiss her, then leave her in the light.
Raising his hand he marks a cross in the air
And turns from her, to hobble toward the dark,
A little room inhabited by fear,
Where powers and principalities may lurk
Which he has struggled to vanquish and overcome
By faith which still moves mountains, one by one.

FRA SLEKT TIL SLEKT"
("from generation to generation")

I minister to him with soap and water,
Rubbing his sores with salve, cleaning him up—
He does not know I am his elder daughter.
Weeping, he drinks confusion's bitter cup.
"Once I was a public man who spoke
So thousands heard me, and to some effect—
I preached salvation so the sleepers woke."
Pulling his diapers on, "Fra slekt til slekt,"
The biblical Norwegian he could preach
Twines with his English in a knotted string.
The old language he never thought to teach
His children, though he taught us many things,
Like how to bend to serve him in his need,
And honor him by holding to his creed.

GRIEF IN THE MONTH OF MARCH

Even the winter dies. Old drifts of snow
Lie strewn like dirty laundry in the yard,
Sad remnants of the fall. The ancient foe
Cannot deceive us in the month of March.
Our ebbing vessels fill and disappear,
The tabernacles of our flesh will fail,
Grief from a hidden spring of salty tears
Will leave us mourning what we cannot tell—
The snow will melt, sending its waters down
The river in a flood nothing can quell,
Washing away roads, bridges, farms and towns—
Turning the frozen spring into a lake,
Sweeping our old foundations in its wake.

BALESTRAND, NORWAY

The poet speaks of beauty as it dies.
The mountains, rivers, seas and hills remain,
They do not die, the day does, as the skies
Change color, turn, and fade, leaving a stain
Of scarlet evenings along the ragged edge
Of cedar covered hills. The water fall
Gushing from the mountain, down a rocky ledge
Crashing into the fjord is musical.
That beauty perishes I understand
More fully than I did when I was young,
The scenery endures, it is my hand
Will grow insensible, death stop my tongue.
Others will mark the shadows, the summer light,
The long red sundown of the Arctic night.

OLD TONGUES

Up against the final enemy
I'll need the old, familiar words, well-worn
No innovations, or revisions will be
Advised. Do not dare to speak them, my scorn
Will arc out like electric fire, and glib tongues stopped
In the mouth. The last journey we all take
Is difficult, frightening, without a map.
Only a low born Judean has come back
With any information I'd dare to trust.
I'll come up wanting if you try to prove
Your qualities against this bag of dust.
Speak the imperishable word to me, remove
My pride and bend me to another's will—
Let it sound like iron tongues against bright steel.

THE POET TO THE LAWYER
(for Audrey)

I think that words are plastic, to be shaped
Into prosodic forms that sing, have edges
Numinous with meanings, lines that try to map
Places cartographers will miss, steep ledges
Where the compass is no help at all—
The mind, the place where human character
Needs help naming the heights from which we fall,
Specific words, lined out, that soar and stir
The human soul. But these are not exact,
They will not stand up in a court of law,
They connote more than statutory fact—
Without your careful work, not worth a straw
Until you came and took my signature
And made it say what I had thought for years.

PURE GRANITE
(For Walter on his 50th birthday)

Under the pressure of their own weight
Even strong buildings break and crack
Folding the plaster over itself, gray slate
Snaps under foot, our flesh balloons and sags
Wrinkled and baggy around our fallible bones.
We walk like living ruins through our days
Feeling the ramparts crack, another stone
Fall from the height, its once unshaken place.
It's grim, they say, the saints who've gone before
Through the dark valley. What you need is faith
And courage, simple courage, not much more
To keep on stepping forward toward your death.
Even pure granite grinds itself down and makes
Powder from every piece of stone it breaks.

THE MARBLE LISTS OF DEATH

The hospital, its marble lists of death
Where every kingdom ends, even the best.
Disease must die, it is an article of faith
We must confess to undergo more tests.
Doctors must kill to cure—the killing fields
My mother's body, shrunken down to bone.
Still monarch over her subjects, she wields
Her scepter. Nothing can topple her from her throne
But death. The battle is fierce, he has the edge—
Her mortal flesh, where he has pitched his tent.
Holding the winning card, she does not hedge
Her bets, she'll lose but once. She's sent
For reinforcements to a greater Lord
Whose treaty she reads daily. She trusts his word.

FEAR OF THE DARK
(the baby boomers say goodbye to their parents)

They are gone now, into the darkness, toward a
    light
We cannot see, but they believe in. The dark
Only a brief but fearful taste of night,
And then the morning. We can only mark
Their time with us on documents with ink,
Scratched out by bored officials whose job it is
To set our great occasions down and link
Our toasts and laughter to the past. The fizz
Of our champagne flattens on the printed page.
This is the way we perish, flesh to dust.
Their names will fade, their grandchildren will age,
As they break like icebergs from the rest of us
And float off into the mists and leave us here
No longer between us and the dark we fear.

ESSENCE AND ACCIDENCE

The mind, once whole, is gone to pieces, shards
Of will and memory reduced to tears.
He's hostage to the whims of unknown lords
Whose goings on outrage him and mock his fears.
His antic brain is desperate to mean,
To pull it all together and make his world
The lovely place it was, his plans and dreams
Laid out in ordered essences, not curled
Like corkscrews in his head. It's when he weeps
Because he cannot recognize his own,
His son and daughters, or his wife, who keeps
Watch over him, knowing we die alone,
You see patience and courage up against
Death, disorder, flesh, his accidence.

GRIEF IN THE MONTH OF MAY
(30 May 1997)

Tears, this is the time for salty tears,
Bursting from aching reservoirs of grief
Stored up over these many days and years
Purging the heart and cleansing it. Relief
Spills toward the air and catches the crystal light
Shining around us in the morning sun.
The end of May, of winter's stony night,
Sings like the lark over his grave. He's gone.
The undertaker stands in his raven suit
Waiting beside the hearse. The flowering plum
Have frittered their blossoms, bent on purple fruit
And a fertile stone. We knew this day would come,
We wished it, even prayed for his release.
Love is the hurt that rises, that cannot cease.

KNEELING TO DUST

Even after he died his hands were warm.
We held them as he breathed his last and said
Together words he taught us from the Psalms.
Blessing him as he'd blessed us with his word
Feeling his restless spirit come to rest,
No longer taut with worry for our sakes.
His ministry is done. Kneeling to dust
Where only weeks ago he knelt to take
Each book from the shelf to carefully wipe it off,
I see his hands lifting each book from its place
Not quite able to handle it, his grief
Because he could not with his native grace
Bring order to the elements he served
Nor raise a benediction to his love.

A DISH OF PENNIES

A dish of pennies spilled over the floor
The day my father died, strewing a path
On which I've walked each day, the copper ore
Glinting under my feet like salt or dust
I cannot shake from my soles, or cast aside.
The ancients, whose randy gods were hard to trust,
Set pennies on a dead man's vacant eyes
To pay the toll across the River Styx.
The boatman would exact his fearful toll
And push toward suffering flesh could not fix.
On earth my father gathered little gold,
He banked on one exchange that made him heir
Of one who took a killing to pay his fare.

GRIEF AT THE END OF AUGUST
(21 August 1997, Lake Superior)

I'm stranger to the company I keep
In this world. Each day I hear my father's song
Lifting inside my head—awake, asleep—
Hymns about pilgrims on their way who long
To see the ending of their journey home,
The one whose promises cannot be broken,
Even though mountains crash from their lofted domes,
Valleys be lifted up. His word, once spoken
Never fails. One day we'll see him face
To face, the object of my father's speech.
When he would bring the sermon home to us
We'd see light breaking within him and want to reach
Forward, and leave whatever stood in our way
Even the glory of this August day.

0-595-21517-3